How many times can you find the word FRIENDS in the puzzle? Look up, down, forward, and backward.

```
P X Z S Y J A C F P
Q B D E F G K L R Q
D M N S P Q O C I D
U D F D E H J I E U
V K M N L O P N N V
B R T E S V U X D B
N F R I E N D S S N
O W Y R Z R A B F O
P G E F D I K C H P
Q J S D N E I R F Q
```

ANSWER: 4.

"These are my BFFs, Teresa and Nikki!"

Teresa is artsy.

Nikki is a great dancer.

Steven is Ken's best bud.

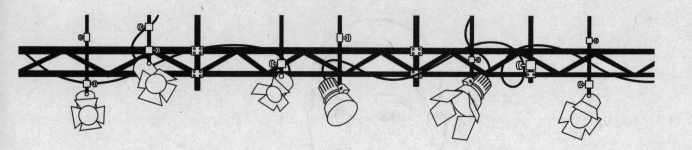

Ryan is Raquelle's brother. He loves to rock out.

Barbie and her friends love to hang out at her house.

Playtime at the pool!

Backyard barbecue!

Barbie loves her friends. Look up, down, forward, and
backward to find Barbie's friends' names.

Teresa • Nikki • Summer • Raquelle
Ken • Steven • Ryan

```
R A N E V E T S C
A D F G E K R U N
Q L N O P M Y M I
U T E R E S A M K
E Q D E F J N E K
L M L N P S T R I
L U W Z G H I J L
E V X M I N T U B
```

Teresa invites Barbie to a party.

Time to shop!

Barbie, Teresa, and Nikki are searching
for the perfect party dresses.

Design your own party dress here.

Beautiful bows.

Bright and bubbly!

Super style!

Barbie's puppy, Lacey, makes the best accessory.

Fun and fancy.

Connect the dots to see which dress Barbie loves.

The perfect dress!

A cut here and a stitch there make a fantastic fit!

Teresa and Nikki try on dazzling dresses.

Barbie loves Teresa's party dress.

Barbie looks at lots of rings.
Create some more rings with jewels.

Sweetheart bracelets.

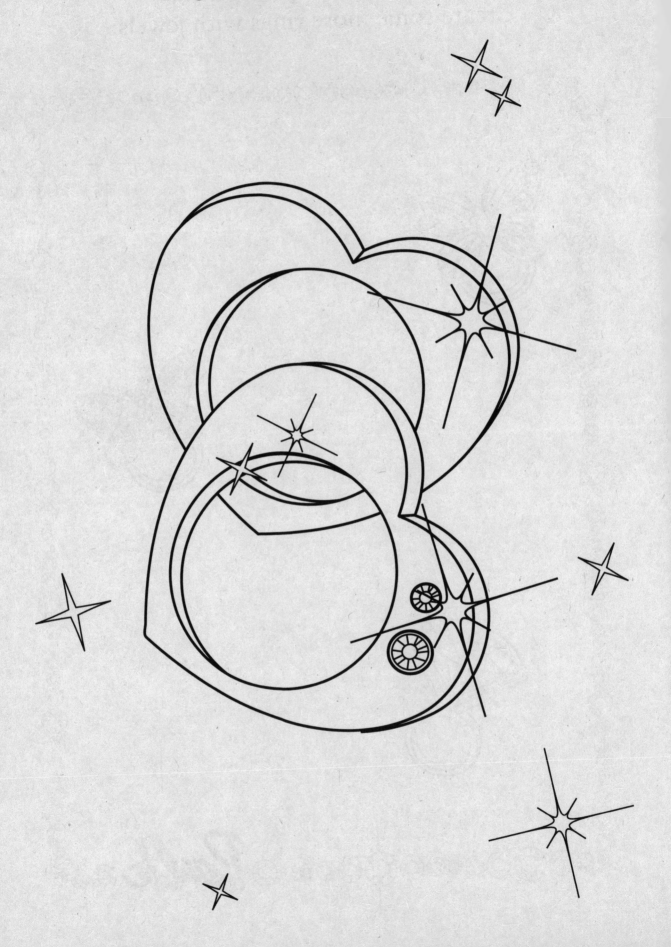

A pretty purse.

Teatime!

Fabulous flowers.

Help Barbie create a bracelet for her BFF Teresa.
Draw a pendant on the chain.

Barbie picks the perfect present for Teresa.

© Mattel

Barbie chooses a cute cake for Teresa's party.

Barbie—and Lacey—can't wait for Teresa's party!

Spa time!

Color Barbie's nails pink.

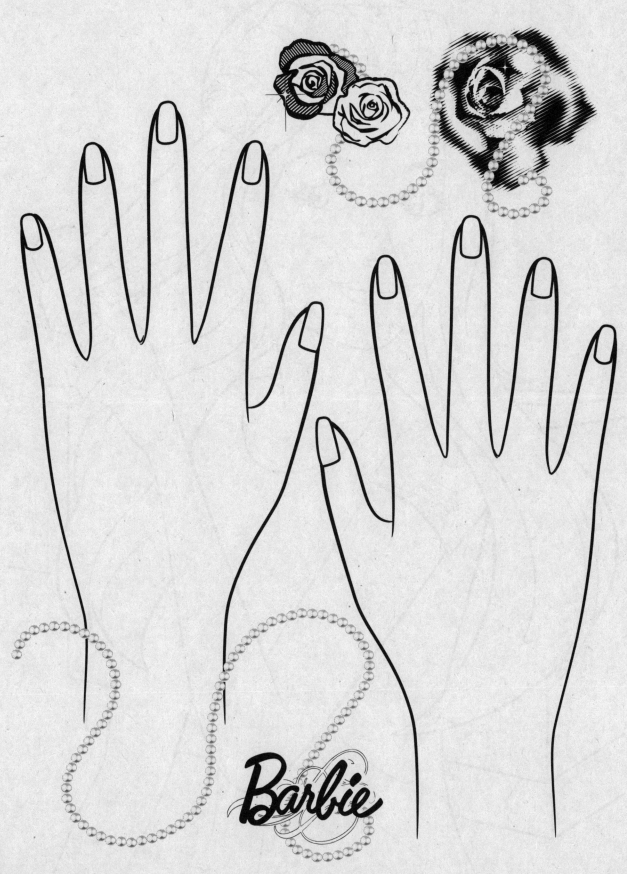

Crazy for curls.

Barbie's pets approve of her party dress.

Nikki and Barbie are ready for the party.

Teresa is so happy to see Barbie.

Connect the dots to see the cute cake creation.

Barbie surprises her friends by joining Ryan
and his band onstage.

Barbie rocks the house!

Time for bed!

Barbie is so excited—the prom is next week!

Barbie hopes Ken will invite her to the dance.

Which gown should Barbie wear?

Nikki and Steven practice some moves.

Ken invites Barbie to the prom!

Barbie gets her hair styled.

Draw your favorite hair accessories on Barbie.

Ken looks so handsome in his tuxedo!

Ken gives Barbie a beautiful bouquet!

Barbie and Ken are late for the prom.
Find the fastest way for them to get there.

START

FINISH

ANSWER:

Barbie and Ken are king and queen of the prom.

Barbie™

Surf's Up!

"Hi! I'm Barbie, and I love the beach."

Look up, down, backward, and forward to find these beach words:

surf • waves • sand • shovel • bucket
shells • starfish • dolphin

```
F B U C K E T B A C
D N I H P L O D E F
M O N G H I L N K J
P Y Z A T S R A S B
Q S T A R F I S H E
G H Q B I U V U O G
F E C D H X Z R V F
E L L R J S W F E T
N L M T K Y A C L U
O S E V A W V W X D
```

ANSWER:

Barbie and Nikki are ready to catch some waves.

Surf's up!

Hang ten!

Barbie's dog, Lacey, hangs twenty!

Barbie boogies on her boogie board.

Catch the wave!

Barbie and Summer make a splash!

Barbie has to meet Ken for lunch. Can you help her find the quickest way back to the beach?

ANSWER:

Beach beauty.

Time for a sweet treat with Ken.

Snack time!

Barbie spikes the ball.

Nikki and Barbie roll along the boardwalk.

Barbie and Nikki hit the waves.

Swimming with the dolphins.

Sealed with a kiss.

Barbie and Ken soak up the sun.

Parasailing over the sea.

Barbie is a waterskiing ace!

Barbie loves the water!

Surfer girls.

Sitting pretty.

Sand castles in the sun.

Barbie draws in the sand.

Draw your favorite beach activity.

Barbie listens to the ocean in her shell.

"I had fun in the sun!"

Seashell Necklace

You will need crayons, scissors, a hole punch, and yarn.
• Color the shells.
• Ask an adult to help you cut out the shells and punch a hole where indicated.
• With an adult's help, cut a piece of yarn about sixteen inches long.
• Thread the yarn through the hole in each shell.
• Ask an adult to tie the two ends of the yarn loosely around your neck.

Barbie™

PRETTY IN PINK!

Barbie is a glamour girl on the go.

Glimmer and shine!

Dance the night away.

Glam and glitz.

Barbie rocks the red carpet.

Getting ready to go.

Dressed to impress.

Cover girl.

Barbie is getting ready to go out, but her shoes are mismatched. Can you help her match her shoes?

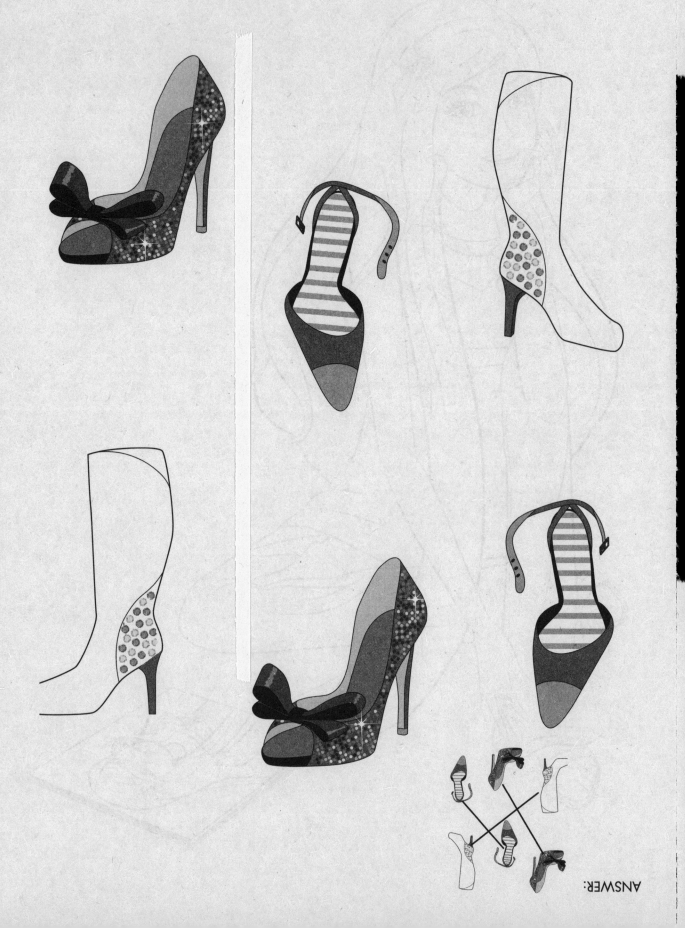

ANSWER:

The perfect fit.

© Mattel

Sparkle and shine.

Dazzling dress.

Time for a touch-up.

Spring into fashion.

Nikki's going dancing!

Pretty as a princess.

Barbie is on her toes!

Getting ready for a party!

© Mattel

All dressed up!

Off to the dance!

Be a dazzling designer.
Decorate a new dress for Barbie.

Teresa is totally cute!

Sunny smile!

Barbie loves roses!

Design your own outfit here.

Guess who?

"I love to dress up!"

Teresa and Barbie find a fluffy friend.

Picture-perfect!

Fashionable friends!

"See you later!"

Barbie™

Think Pink!

Barbie is cool and casual.

Sitting pretty.

Fabulous friends.

Ready on the set!

Friends forever.

Barbie loves pets.

Backstage VIP.

School cool.

Out for a ride!

Great book!

Ready to rock!

School style.

On the town.

Barbie™

Pink Sand and Sunshine!

Barbie loves to have fun in the sun.

Surfer girls.

Beach beauty.

Can you find the five differences between this page and the facing one? Circle them.

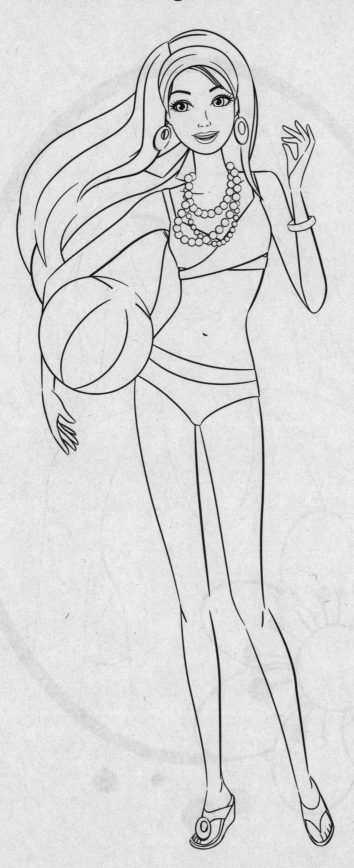

ANSWER: On this page, Barbie is missing her sunglasses, the round charm on her necklace is gone, a bracelet is gone, the circle on the ball is gone, and Barbie has a charm on one sandal.

Sun-sational!

Bunches of bracelets.

Circle all the things Barbie will need to have fun in the sun.

Playtime!

Sunny days.

Pretty as a picture!

A day at the beach.

Terrific trio!

Having a ball!

Sweet and stylish.

Sunshine and smiles.

Barbie™

Spring into Style

"Hi! I'm Barbie, and I love spring!"

Fabulous flowers.

Connect the dots to see what Barbie is holding.

Jump to it!

Go, go, Barbie!

Barbie's dog, Lacey, is ready for a long walk in the sun.

LOVE Barbie

Off to the pet park.

Spring bling.

As sweet as a spring day.

Bunches of bracelets.

Ready for the spring fashion show.

How many times can you find the word SPRING in the puzzle below?

```
B D F G S K Y L
G N I R P S A C
M N S P R I N G
T O H J I L K N
J P T S N V W I
M I L K G J U R
K S J V U P F P
S P R I N G D S
```

ANSWER: 5.

Snow cones on a sunny day.

Flower girl.

Out for a ride.

Unscramble the letters to make spring words.

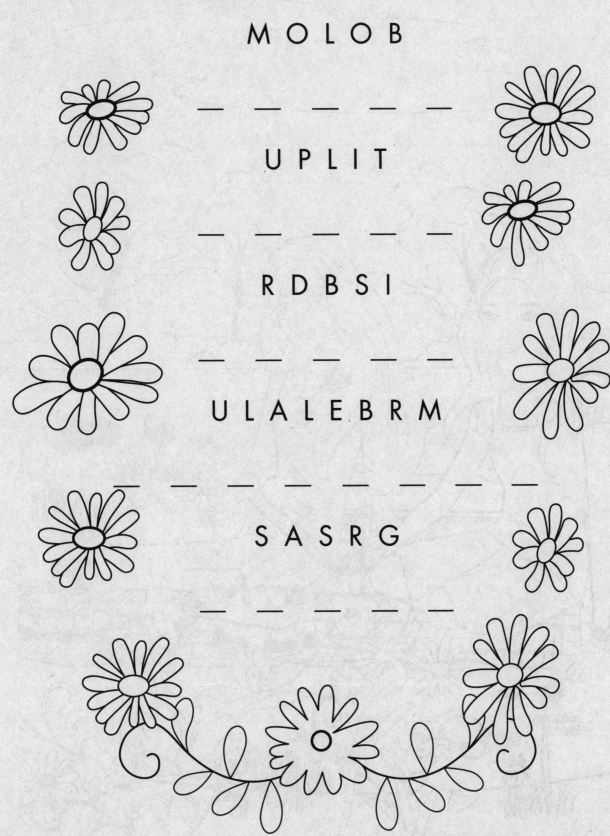

M O L O B

_ _ _ _ _

U P L I T

_ _ _ _ _

R D B S I

_ _ _ _ _

U L A L E B R M

_ _ _ _ _ _ _ _

S A S R G

_ _ _ _ _

ANSWER: Bloom, tulip, birds, umbrella, and grass.

Tea for two.

Bubbly beauties.

Hooray for spring!

Rock 'n' roll!

Great catch!

Anyone for tennis?

Cute and cuddly!

I may be too cute for some people!

Teresa and Barbie spring into action.

Spring break!

Spring sleepover.

Splish, splash!

FLOWER NECKLACE

You will need crayons, scissors, a hole punch, and yarn.
- Color the flowers.
- Ask an adult to help you cut out the flowers and punch a hole where indicated.
- With an adult's help, cut a piece of yarn about sixteen inches long.
- Thread the yarn through the hole in each flower.
- Ask an adult to tie the two ends of the yarn loosely around your neck.

Barbie and Teresa pick pretty daisies.

Caught in a spring shower.

Come sail away!

A *purr*-fect sunny day!

Barbie loves to swing in the shade.

Circle the picture of Barbie that is different.

A

B

C

D

E

Cool spring fashions!

The *purr*-fect pets.

Queen of the spring dance.

Sequin and Barbie are ready for a sunny day.

Which handbag do you like the best?

Teresa and Barbie have a spring in their step.

Paris is beautiful in the springtime.

Beauty in bloom.

Spring surprise!

Girls on the go!

Spring concert in the park.

Time for a spring makeover.

Breezy style!

Beautiful bouquet.

Fun at the fair.

Time for a sweet treat!

Barbie has spring fever.

Spring style.

Barbie is the star of the spring ballet recital!

Happy spring!